Don't Think About Purple Elephants

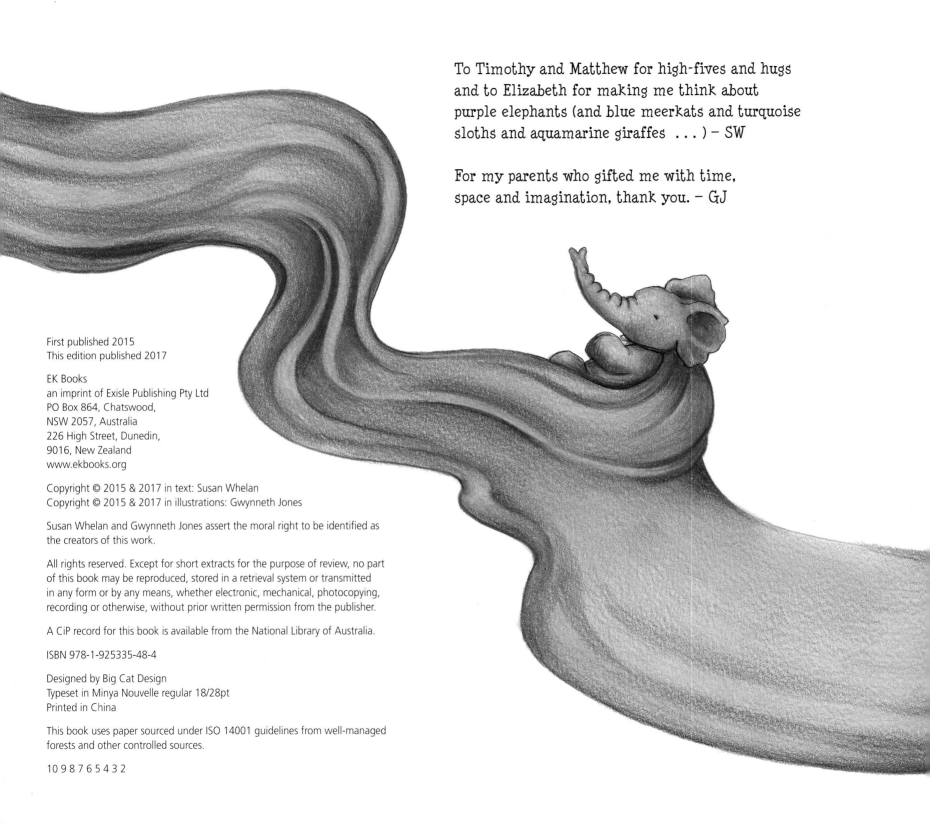

To Timothy and Matthew for high-fives and hugs
and to Elizabeth for making me think about
purple elephants (and blue meerkats and turquoise
sloths and aquamarine giraffes . . .) — SW

For my parents who gifted me with time,
space and imagination, thank you. — GJ

First published 2015
This edition published 2017

EK Books
an imprint of Exisle Publishing Pty Ltd
PO Box 864, Chatswood,
NSW 2057, Australia
226 High Street, Dunedin,
9016, New Zealand
www.ekbooks.org

A CiP record for this book is available from the National Library of Australia.

ISBN 978-1-925335-48-4

Designed by Big Cat Design
Typeset in Minya Nouvelle regular 18/28pt
Printed in China

This book uses paper sourced under ISO 14001 guidelines from well-managed
forests and other controlled sources.

10 9 8 7 6 5 4 3 2

Don't Think About Purple Elephants

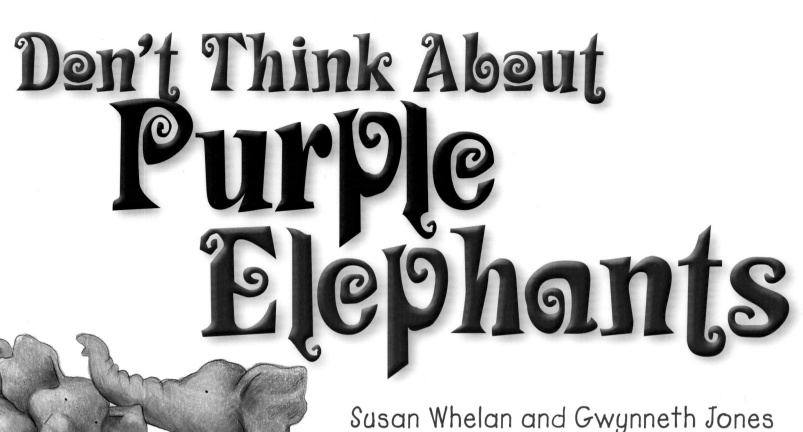

Susan Whelan and Gwynneth Jones

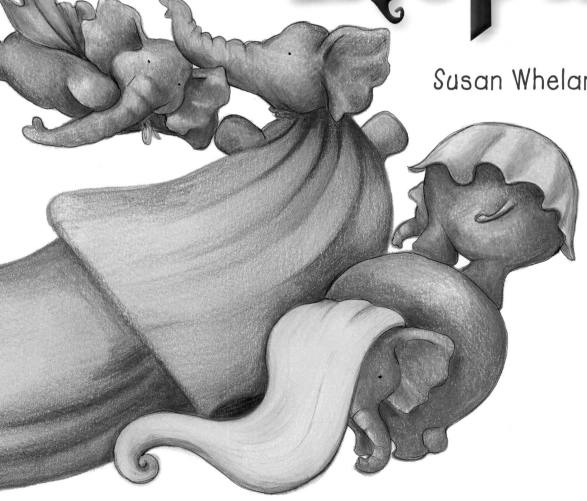

Sometimes Sophie worried.

She didn't worry on weekdays when she went to school, where she learned all sorts of interesting things and played with her friends.

She didn't worry in the afternoons when she played games and drew pictures.

She didn't worry on weekends when she read
books, baked cakes, helped in the garden ...

... rode her bike and lay on the grass looking at clouds.

During the day Sophie was busy thinking about all the fun things she was doing, but at bedtime, when everything was quiet and still and there were no games to play or lessons to learn, Sophie started to worry.

What if they ran out of milk and she
couldn't have cereal for breakfast?

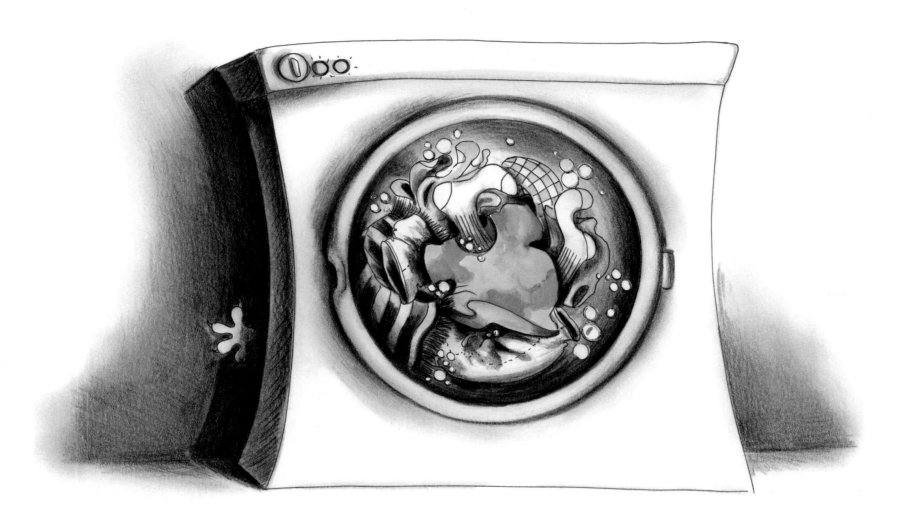

What if her favourite shirt was still in the wash and she couldn't wear it on the weekend?

What if she forgot her lunch
and had nothing to eat at school?

What if Mum cooked Brussels sprouts for dinner? (Sophie didn't like Brussels sprouts.)

Sophie's worries made it hard for her to get to sleep and she was often tired in the mornings. Sometimes she was so tired, she couldn't do all the things she loved to do.

Her family tried to help.

Oliver loaned Sophie his favourite book for a bedtime story, but the cover gave her new things to worry about.

Emily gave Sophie her teddy, but Sophie
worried that her little sister wouldn't be able
to sleep without him, so she gave teddy a quick
cuddle and put him back on Emily's bed.

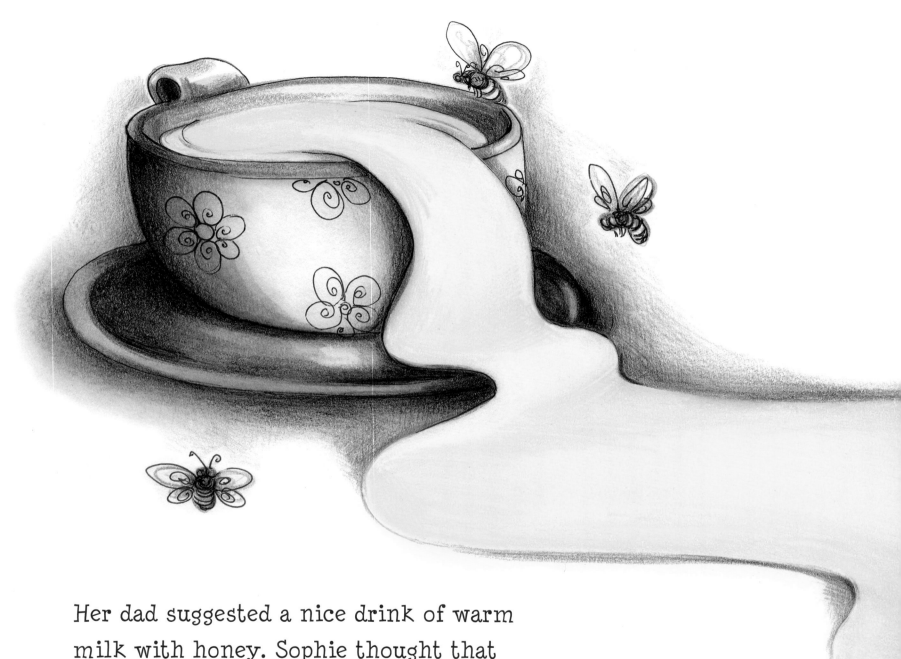

Her dad suggested a nice drink of warm milk with honey. Sophie thought that sounded delicious, but she worried she would need to go to the toilet during the night (or maybe she might wet the bed).

What was Sophie going to do? She
was so sleepy, but every time she
closed her eyes she started to worry.

'I know,' said Mum. 'Go to bed, close your eyes
and DON'T think about purple elephants. No cute
little purple elephants, no big purple elephants
at the circus. No purple elephants at all.'

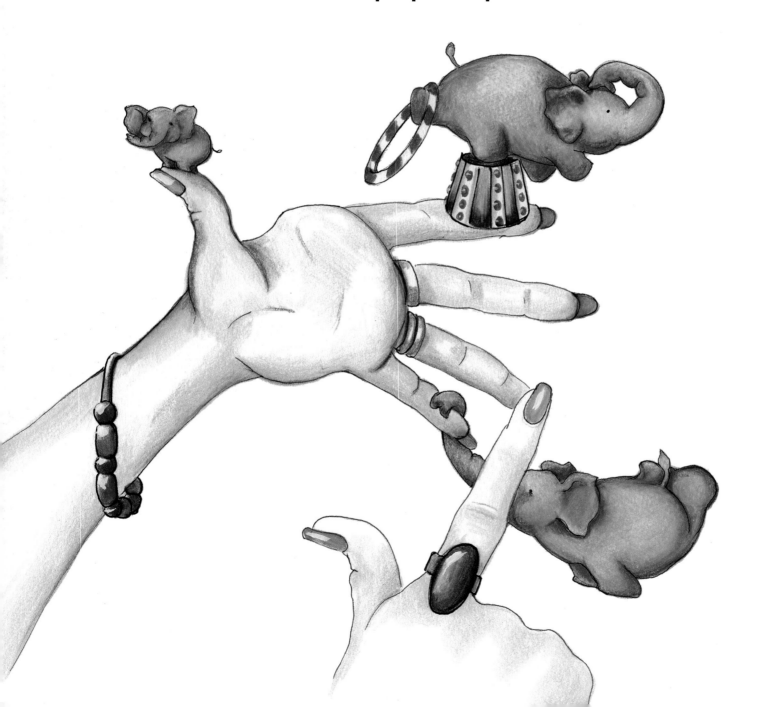

'How silly,' thought Sophie, but she lay down, closed her eyes and tried to not think about purple elephants.

Straight away a friendly purple elephant appeared in her mind.

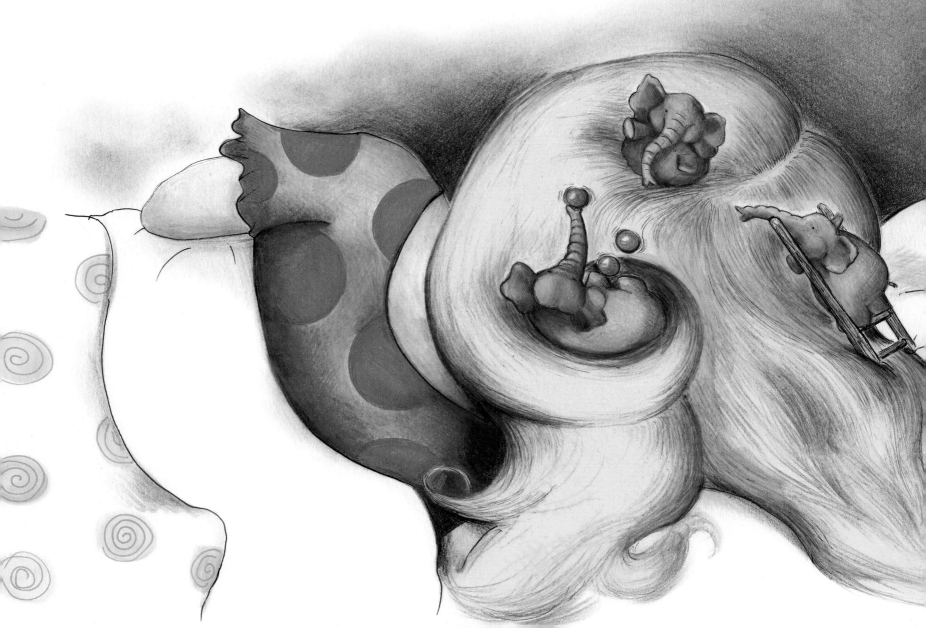

Then another and another until purple elephants were all Sophie could think about.

Sophie smiled at the funny things the
elephants were doing and slowly drifted
off to sleep, her worries forgotten.

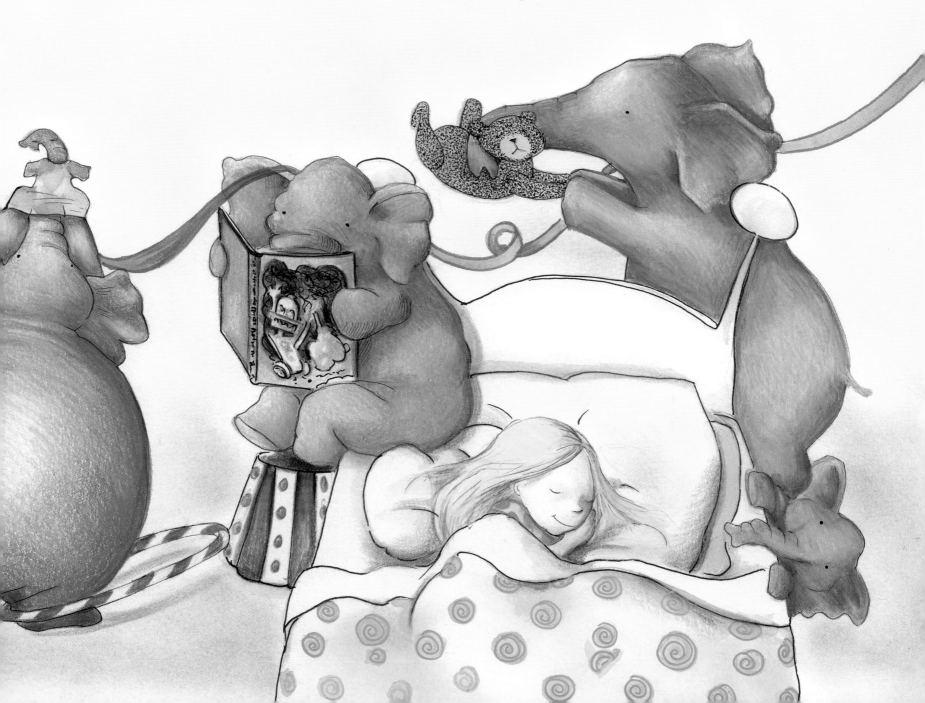

The next day, when Sophie woke up she wasn't tired. She had fun with her friends at school, played games with Oliver and Emily in the afternoon and drew some pictures of purple elephants.

When Mum came in to kiss Sophie at bedtime that night, Sophie said 'I don't need to not think about purple elephants tonight.' 'Really?' said Mum.

'No. Tonight I'm going to not think about blue monkeys,' said Sophie with a smile and she closed her eyes.

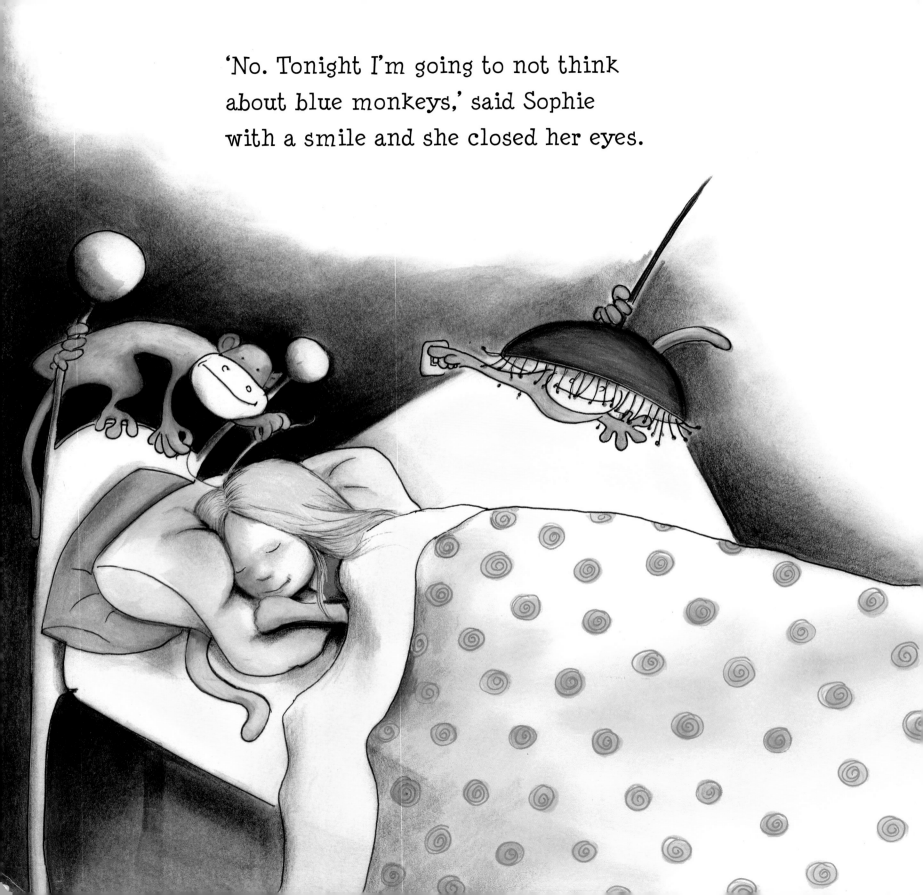